IR 4.2/05

BASKETBALL: PASS, SHOOT & DRIBBLE

BRYANT LLOYD

The Rourke Book Co., Inc.
Vero Beach, Florida 32964

PHOTO CREDITS
cover, p. 6, 10, 15, 20 © Andrew Young; p. 9, 12, 13, 16, 18 © Bryant Lloyd; p. 4, 7, 19, 22 courtesy Beacon News, Aurora, IL

EDITORIAL SERVICES:
Penworthy Learning Systems

Library of Congress Cataloging-in-Publication Data

Lloyd, Bryant. 1942
    Basketball: pass, shoot & dribble / by Bryant Lloyd.
       p. cm. — (Basketball)
    Includes index
    Summary: Provides an overview of the three basic skills necessary in the game of basketball: passing, dribbling, and shooting.
       ISBN 1-55916-227-9
    1. Basketball—Juvenile literature. [1. Basketball.]
1. Title II. Series: Lloyd, Bryant, 1942- Basketball.
    GV885.1.L56 1997
    796.323—dc21   97–8438
                                                                                         CIP
                                                                                          AC

Printed in the USA

TABLE OF CONTENTS

SKILLS OF THE GAME

Basketball players need special skills to play the game. Three of those skills are being able to pass, shoot, and **dribble** (DRIB ul) a basketball.

Dribble is another word for bounce. A basketball player who is moving with the ball must dribble it with one hand.

The player moving with the ball doesn't have to dribble when he or she drives toward the basket. The player can take the last running step or two without a dribble.

A player takes the hook shot with his or her pivot, or turning, foot planted on the floor. With a jump hook, the player takes the hook shot as he or she jumps.

A good dribbler can move closer to the basket by slipping past defenders.

PASSING THE BALL

A player can move a basketball toward the team's basket by dribbling or passing. A pass is a throw of the ball from one teammate to another.

By moving without the ball, as No. 35 is doing, a player can shake free for a pass from a teammate.

Throwing an off-balance pass from the floor is tough, and it is likely to be grabbed by someone from the other team.

By passing, a player can move the ball a great distance in a very short time. A quick pass to a teammate who is not closely guarded often results in a basket.

When passing, a player steps toward the direction of the throw.

LOW PASSES

Young basketball players usually pass the ball by one of three ways: the chest pass, bounce pass, or overhead pass. Each pass is useful in a different game situation.

A chest pass is a throw using two hands from the chest area. The bounce pass is usually a two-handed throw of the ball from about waist high. A bounce pass is thrown to strike the floor and bounce into the hands of a teammate.

Player avoids defender with a chest pass. Passing the basketball moves it faster than dribbling.

HIGH PASSES

The overhead pass is thrown with two hands from over the head. A player throws the ball forward with a snap of his or her wrists.

Older players sometimes throw a long, one-handed pass. It is called a baseball pass. It is thrown with the same overhand motion used to throw a baseball.

When catching a pass, a player uses two hands and steps towards the pass. He or she should meet the ball, not wait for it.

For a hook shot, a player flips the ball over his or her head toward the basket. The motion often begins underhanded, but finishes overhanded. The shot is usually taken close to the basket, most often from the lane.

The "baseball" pass is an overhand throw, usually used for a long pass.

DRIBBLING

Dribbling a basketball helps an offensive player move past defensive players.

A low-control dribble works best when the ball handler is guarded closely. The ball handler keeps the bounce low, close to his or her body. The dribbler's free hand should reach out to help protect the ball.

Low-control dribble is easier to keep than a high dribble, but a dribbler can't move as fast when crouched for a low dribble.

Dribbler should never try to take on two defensive players. This ball handler, who's being double-teamed, should look to pass.

A high-control, or speed, dribble can be used when the player is not closely guarded. The high-dribble bounce is about waist high.

On any dribble, the player must be careful to keep the dribbling hand palm down.

SHOOTING

Throwing the basketball into the basket scores points. A player who throws the ball toward the basket in an attempt to score is a **shooter** (SHOO ter). The throw is a **shot** (SHOT).

Most shots are jump shots. A jump shooter lifts the ball up with two hands. The ball rests on the left hand if the shooter is right-handed.

As the player jumps, facing the basket, he or she releases the ball. A right-handed shooter pushes the ball up toward the basket with a snap of the right wrist.

Players once shot their free throws underhanded, using both hands. NBA great Rick Barry, in the 1970's, was the last of the professional players to shoot free throws that way.

Basketball players shoot jump shots most of the time. As a player jumps, he or she releases the ball from the shooting hand.

SHOTS

Another shot is the **lay-up** (LAY UP), or lay-in. A lay-up is a shot taken from as close to the basket as a player can be. A lay-up often comes at the end of a player's dribble and run to the basket.

The hook shot is taken close to the basket, too, but normally from about eight to twelve feet (about 2 1/2 meters to 3 1/2 meters) away. It is a sweeping, overhand shot. It is taken with the shooter's side facing the basket.

The dunk, or slam, is an exciting shot. A leaping player slams the ball into the basket from above the rim.

A player soars and lays the ball on the backboard glass, just above the rim, for a layup and two points.

PICKING THE RIGHT SHOT

Knowing when not to shoot is as important as knowing when to shoot. A player needs to be in rhythm—be comfortable—to shoot. While a player is stumbling or feeling unsure is not a good time to shoot.

Shooter fires a shot over defender. Knowing when to shoot helps a shooter score.

Coach shows his team the proper way to shoot free throws. Free throw shooters don't take jump shots.

A player should be close enough to the basket for a reasonable chance at making the shot. At the same time, the shooter should have at least an arm's distance between him or herself and a defensive player.

FREE THROW SHOOTING

A **free throw** (FREE THRO) is a shot from a line 15 feet (about 4 1/2 meters) from the backboard. The line is directly in front of the basket.

Free throws are awarded to players in certain situations after they have been **fouled** (FOWLD).

The free throw shot is almost always a one-handed set shot. The player shoots from a set position instead of jumping.

For free throws, feet should be set slightly wider than the shoulders. A right-hander's right foot should be set slightly forward of the left.

A hook shot is taken as the player stands sideways to the basket. The player can see the basket by turning his or her head.

About to practice a free throw, or foul shot, player carefully eyes basket.

GLOSSARY

dribble (DRIB ul) — to bounce a basketball with the hand, palm down; the bouncing of the basketball by a player

fouled (FOWLD) — to have been charged, slapped, blocked, or pushed illegally on a basketball court

free throw (FREE THRO) — a shot awarded to a player from the 15-foot (about 4 1/2 meters) distance after a foul against that player

lay-up (LAY UP) — a basket scored by laying the ball into the basket from very close range

shooter (SHOO ter) — the player who throws the ball towards the basket in an attempt to score

shot (SHOT) — a throw towards the basket in an attempt to score

A high school player finishes off a slam dunk. For a dunk, player must raise the ball above the rim and slam it through the basket.

INDEX